I AM....
(Positive Affirmations For Brown Boys)

By Ayesha Rodriguez

This book
is for

_____

From

_____

Library of Congress Cataloging-in-Publication Data
ISBN: 978-1-4951-9564-8 (sc)
ISBN: 978-1-4951-9567-9 (hc)

Publisher Jaye Squared Youth Empowerment Services, INC.
Website: www.ayesharodriguez.com

Illustration copyright © 2016 by Rina Risnawati

Layout Design by Susan Gulash
Gulash Graphics, Lutz, FL

This book is dedicated to all of you wonderfully made brown boys. I may not know you all personally, but I support and believe in you.

TABLE OF CONTENTS

Amazing men have come before me. I will be one too.

Following in their footsteps is something I must do.

I am great.

I look to history as one of my biggest teachers.

I am proud of my brown complexion and my African features.

I am handsome.

I am happy with myself for doing
the right things.

Being honest, caring and fair
give me good feelings.

I am kind.

Doing my best in school is something I will do.

Learning math and science is pretty awesome too!

I am smart.

I eat healthy foods and exercise a lot.

I have to be good to my body, it's the only one I've got!

I am important.

Family and friends want
me to succeed.

Even those I don't know, support
and believe in me.

I am loved.

I can be president, a professor, or even have my own business!

It takes a lot of hard work, but I know that I can do this!

I am able.

I am a reflection of God and
He lives within me.

I come from excellence. I will
fulfill my destiny.

I am thankful.

I am great.
I am handsome.
I am kind.
I am smart.
I am important.
I am loved.
I am able.
I am thankful.

I am a King.

Daily Activity:

Stand in the mirror every day and repeat all of the sentences that start with the words "I am". I want you to really believe it, just like I do! If people say things to you that are not nice, you will know in your heart that it is not true!

You are amazing and I'm so proud of you.

Discussion Questions:

1. Who do you think is an amazing man?

2. What makes him so special?

3. What do you love about yourself?

4. He is holding a book in his hands. Why do you think the book says untold history?

5. How do you feel when you do the right thing?

6. What makes you happy?

7. What subjects do you like to learn about?

8. Are you doing your best in school?

9. Can you tell me some healthy foods that you like?

10. What exercises do you like to do?

11. What does love mean to you?

12. What are you thankful for?

13. Practice makes perfect! What are some things that you need to work harder on?

Are there more affirmations that you would like
to add? Write them in pencil below.

1. I am_____

2. I am_____

3. I am_____

4. I am_____

5. I am_____

6. I am_____

7. I am_____

8. I am_____

About the Author

Ayesha Rodriguez is the president of a 501c3 children's nonprofit organization, entrepreneur, author, speaker and most importantly, a mother of two. She is very passionate about education and making a positive impact in the community.

CPSIA information can be obtained
at www.ICGtesting.com
Printed in the USA
LVHW071542080121
675967LV00008B/561